USEFULNESS OF HERBS

BENEFITS OF CULINARY HERBS

BY WILLIAMS BROOK

TABLE OF CONTENTS

EXPERIENCE

PREFACE

A young kid once took his little sweetheart to an ice cream shop to impress her. Say, Mister, what you got that looks tiny and tastes nice for nineteen cents? he whispered to the waiter after fruitlessly searching the list of edibles for something within his price range.

Many thousands of people are currently in the same situation. They share the boy's tight wallets, ravenous appetites, and fierce yearnings to leave the best impression they can. Perhaps after being invited out, they witness firsthand how the herbs work their culinary magic to transform cheap cuts and trash into delectable hors d'oeuvres. They are thus alerted to the fact that they can afford it by taking herbs.

INTRODUCTION TO CULINARY HERBS

How delightfully we turn away from the dull repetition of the tiny menu in these days of jaded appetites, sauces, and canned products to the memories of the filling dishes of our moms! Why did we demand more, just like Oliver Twist? Were those flavors there, or were we just drawn in by association and our natural, young hunger? Can we ever forget them, or, more practically, can we ever come to understand them once more? Mother's garden may hold the key and the solution. Peep inside.

Except for its orderliness and possibly the blending of flowers, fruits, and vegetables—which we never see on the table—the garden is not very noteworthy as we recall it. potatoes, carrots and currants, strawberries, and onions.

[Illustration: Spading Fork]

These are all well-known faces, but what are those plants by the kitchen for? They are sweet herbs from the mother. They've never been on a table, either. They never had the starring roles that the potato and the cabbage had. They are the only participants in the cast who played little but crucial roles in the creation of the appetizing ensemble soup, stew, sauce, or salad, the memory of which lingers long after the performers have been forgotten, much like the memory of a well-staged and well-performed drama.

[Illustration: Barrel Culture of Herbs]

No culinary plants have likely been neglected as much over the past 50 years. They suffered the most, particularly during the campaign against ready-to-serve meals in the previous quarter century. However, they are once more starting to shine. Very few plants are as simple to grow and prepare for usage. Except for onions, no other ingredient may be used so skillfully or totally to convert leftovers that they lure an ordinarily hesitant appetite to eat another dish without being compelled to fulfill the domestic responsibility of eating it to preserve it. Sweet herbs are or should be, a blessing for housewives because they are economical and pleasurable. The soup may contain just the healthiest and most nourishing.

[**Illustration: Transplanting Board and Dibble**]

By candling the flavorful roots of lovage, one can expand the variety of homemade sweets in a very attractive way and create a competitor for the candied ginger that is rumored to be imported from the Orient. If someone enjoys coriander and caraway, I must confess that I do not enjoy the cane sugar used to manufacture those tiny comforts, the candies from our youth that our moms attempted to convince us to enjoy either independently or when added to our birthday cakes. That was back when each piece didn't have someone's name stamped on it to help with digestion. Can we ever forget the picnic when we ate particular sandwich varieties? The soft sage leaves, marjoram, or other herbs were minced by our mothers and combined with cream cheese before being sandwiched between two thin pieces of bread. It's possible that the swimming, the three-legged races, the swinging, or all of these activities combined sharpened our appetites and caused us to savor those sandwiches more than was perhaps appropriate, but will not all of us who ate them be prepared to refute any claims that the flavors were the reason we forgot to be polite?

However, sweet herbs can also be used for more aesthetically pleasant purposes. Many of them are ornamental. A bouquet of delicate marjoram flowers, pale pink thyme blossoms, and lemon balm sprigs blended with bright yellow sweet fennel umbels, finely divided rue leaves, and long glassy bergamot leaves are not unique in look but also scent. Even sweet peas and roses can't compare to it for deliciousness. A beautiful and long-lasting bouquet that serves as a fragrant reminder of Shakespeare's lines from A Winter's Tale may be created by combining the bright red berries of barberry and multiflora rose with the dark-green branches of hardy thyme, which remains fresh and pleasant throughout the year.

Flowers are here for you;

Hot lavender, mints, savory, and marjoram; a marigold that rises weeping with the sun after going to bed with him.

Many muslin bags of dried leaves delivered to town for stuffing fowl never even make it to the kitchen since the uncommon perfume of sweet marjoram recalls so many city dwellers of their mothers' and grandmothers' country gardens, giving the living room more honorable placements. They are positioned under a bay window's natural light so that Old Sol can free their imprisoned scents and fill the air with the aroma of summers spent on the farm as a child.

Other memories cling to the delicate little lavender, more so because of more tender memories than because the owner of a well-stocked linen closet perfumed her pristine hoard with its fragrant blooms. Without its tiny silk bags packed with dried lavender buds and blooms to provide the final touch of romanticism to the small trousseau of linen and lace, would any country wedding box be complete? What else can so accurately recall the year of the wedding?

A DINNER OF HERBS

In an article published by American Agriculturist, Dora M. Morrell says: There is an inference that a dinner of herbs is rather a poor thing, one not to be chosen as a pleasure. Perhaps it might be if it came daily, but, for once in a while, try this which I am going to tell you.

To prepare a dinner of herbs in its best estate you should have a bed of seasonings such as our grandmothers had in their gardens, rows of sage, spicy mint, sweet marjoram, summer savory, fragrant thyme, tarragon, chives, and parsley. To these, we may add, if we take herbs in the Scriptural sense, nasturtium, and that toothsome esculent, the onion, as well as lettuce. If you wish a dinner of herbs and do have not the fresh, the dried will serve, but parsley and mint you can get at most times in the markets, or in country gardens, where they often grow wild.

Do you know, my sister housewife, that if you were to have a barrel sawed in half, filled with good soil, some holes made in the side, and then placed the prepared half barrel in the sun, you could have an herb garden of your own the year through, even if you live in a city flat? In the holes at the sides, you can plant parsley, and it will grow to cover the barrel so that you have a bank of green to look upon. On the top of the half barrel plant your mint, sage, thyme, and tarragon. Thyme is so pleasing a plant in appearance and fragrance that you may acceptably give it a place among those you have in your window for ornament.

[Illustration: Assortment of Favorite Weeders]

The Belgians produce parsley soup that could start your luncheon or evening. When making the soup, combine the flour and butter to make a drawn butter sauce, and when it is fully cooked, add milk to thin it to soup consistency. Add salt, pepper, and onion juice for flavor. Add enough finely chopped parsley right before serving to turn the soup green. Serve this with croutons.

Opt for an omelet with fine herbs as your main meal. The instructions for creating the omelet may be found in any cookbook, and all that is required in addition to what the book instructs is to add minced thyme, tarragon, and chives before folding the omelet or to stir them in before cooking.

[Illustration: Popular Adjustable Row Marker]

I'm afraid you'll have to look outside of herbs for a dessert. With a silver knife, mash any one or two of these herbs into cream cheese and serve it with toasted crackers. Alternatively, you could toast your crackers with regular cheese while grating sage and thyme on top.

Whether or not the reader finds this dinner of herbs appealing, I dare to say that no housewife who has ever stuffed a Thanksgiving turkey, a Christmas goose, ducks, or chickens with homegrown, home-prepared herbs, either fresh or dried, will ever again be willing to buy the paper packages or tin cans of semi-in odorous, prehistoric dust which masquerades as herbs.

CULINARY HERBS DEFINED

Sweet or culinary herbs can be defined as annual, biennial, or perennial plants that have green parts, tender roots, or ripe seeds that have an aromatic flavor and fragrance. This flavor and fragrance may be caused by a volatile oil or by other chemically named substances that are specific to each species. Many of them have pleasant aromas, so they are referred to as sweet. They are also known as culinary because they have long been used in cooking to add their distinctive flavors to soups, stews, dressings, sauces, and salads. Since many other herbs, like cabbage, spinach, kale, dandelion, and collards, are also culinary herbs, the latter classification is less satisfying than the former. However, these veggies are perhaps more well-known as greens or herbs.

HISTORY

It appears likely that many of the flavoring herbs currently in use were also used in similar ways before the construction of the pyramids, and many of those that were popular at the time are no longer found on modern lists of esculents. This assertion is, of course, largely based on faulty records and, in many cases, merely vague indications of diverse species. But it seems safe to assume that a significant number of the plants discussed in this book, particularly those that are thought to be native to the Mediterranean region, overhung and perfumed the cradle of the human race in the Orient and left traces of our primitive ancestors' footsteps as they walked steadily and resolutely toward the promise of the future.

[**Illustration: Popular Spades**]

The growth of the herb crops differs significantly from that of the other crops mentioned earlier. The former has fallen to the lowest place among all food plants, whilst the latter have remained mainstays and, based on their behavior over the past century, may be deemed to have improved in quality and yield since that ancient time. They have fewer species and perhaps have improved less than any other group of plants that are farmed for economic gain. Only one species, parsley, may be stated to have improved more than just a single variation over the past century. Additionally, it appears that the list of species has been somewhat reduced even during this time.

Except for these few species, whose extinction doesn't seem to be particularly important, this lack of progress is regrettable because the higher quality would encourage greater consumption, which would enhance the delectable flavor of foods that include herbs. However, until a just appreciation has been aroused in individual cultivators—who, most likely, will be plant enthusiasts rather than men who make a living by market gardening—greatly enhanced variations of the majority of species can hardly be expected.

There will be a relatively low commercial demand until consumers are more aware of the benefits of culinary herbs; market gardeners will devote their time to producing herbs until the demand is high enough to make it profitable to do so on a large scale.

Therefore, one of the main goals of this book is to encourage a fair appreciation of the potential available to herb growers. Many people would find positive enjoyment in the breeding of plants for improvement and the origination of new varieties and would devote much of their free time to this work making it a hobby did they know the simple underlying principles. These people would join the very large and growing number of people who take pleasure in the growing of attractive flowering and foliage plants, fine vegetables, and choice fruits. Therefore, the following passages are provided for their benefit.

PRODUCTION OF NEW VARIETY

In addition to the satisfaction that comes with growing plants, plant breeding offers the promise that the offspring will in some way be superior to the parents, as well as the assurance that once a stable variety with undeniable merit has been produced, it can be sold to an astute seedsman for widespread distribution. The amateur can benefit society in this way, receive reasonable compensation for his efforts, and preserve his memory. Contrary to popular belief, creating new plant kinds is a lot simpler procedure. The best specimens are chosen, and those are then multiplied, rather than any so-called breeding. This is the most likely direction in which to move with the majority of the herbs.

[**Illustration: Lath Screen for Shading Beds**]

Assume we have moved 1,000 seedlings to the location where they will develop and produce leaves for consumption or sale. At least 90% of these will be similar in look, production, and other factors if the seed was excellent and true. The surviving plants could have dramatic variances that draw notice. Others may be light green, still others dark green, and so on. Some may be tall and scraggly, others may be small and puny. However, there can be one or two plants that stand out as being the best of the bunch. These are the people that need to be marked with a stake so that they won't be harmed when the crop is picked and that they can achieve theirs.

The same criteria are used to choose the seedlings as in the first year; the best are preferred for transplantation. It is possible to anticipate numerous differences in the bedding that is even more evident than in the first year. Finding the seedlings that most closely resemble each parent plant should be the goal when working with the seedlings that each parent plant produced. These plants should then be managed similarly to the parents. Nobody else should be permitted to bloom.

This procedure must be continued annually. If the choice is thoughtfully made, the grower will soon be jubilant as he sees an increasing number of plants moving toward the kind of plant he has been choosing for.

STATUS AND USES

Some readers with a statistical bent may be disappointed to learn that data on the annual crop prices of specific herbs, the area allocated to each, the average cost, yield, and profit per acre, etc., are not available and that the only way to estimate the relative popularity of the various species is to look at the apparent demand for each in the major markets and retailers.

The biggest need is undoubtedly for parsley, which is used as a garnish in restaurants and hotels more frequently than any other herb. It is comparable to lettuce and watercress in this regard, both of which are primarily used in salads. It is probably used more often than sage, but less frequently, as a flavoring agent.

NOTABLE INSTANCES OF USE

The flavors of the various herbs range widely and can be used in a variety of dishes, starting with fennel and ending with sage. In one instance that I observed, the cook turned some leftover pork into a celery-flavored stew. Not completely devoured, the leftover debris reappeared a day or two later, together with other miscellaneous items, as the star of a parsley-flavored beef pie. But alas, another leftover! Never mind, thought the cook, and no one who ate the stew that followed saw the hidden parsley and its overpowering parent, celery, under the convincing cover of summer savor. Due to an unexpected event, the leftover pieces from this last stew did not complete the cycle and vanished.

METHODS OF CURING

The three categories of culinary herbs include those whose leaves provide flavor, those whose seeds are consumed, and the select few whose roots are cooked. The use of leafy herbs in the kitchen can be done in a variety of ways, each with its benefits, uses, and advocates.

When properly and newly harvested, green herbs are the most flavorful, and, when added to sauces, fricassees, stews, and other dishes, both their particles and their noticeably finer flavor help to indicate how fresh they are. Since their vibrant colors are pleasing to the eye and their crispness to the palate, they almost entirely replace both the dried and the decocted herbs in salads.

The flavors of foliar herbs are invariably best in well-developed leaves and shoot remaining in the full vigor of growth, no matter in what condition or for what purpose they are to be utilized. These flavors are most plentiful and enjoyable for the plant as a whole shortly before the blooms emerge. Additionally, they are more prevalent in the morning than after the sun has reached its zenith since they are typically caused by essential oils, which are swiftly destroyed by heat. The harvest should be done as soon as the dew has dried and before the sun sets to achieve the greatest results with foliar herbs, especially those that will be used for drying and infusing.

[Illustration: Herb Solution Bottle]

Tarragon, mint, and the seed herbs, such as dill, are perhaps more often used in ordinary cookery as infusions than otherwise. An objection to decoctions is that the flavor of vinegar is not always desired in culinary preparation, and neither is that of alcohol or wine, which are sometimes used in the same way as vinegar.

TRANSPLANTING

No more care is required in transplanting herbs than in resetting other plants, but unless a few essentials are realized in practice the results are sure to be unsatisfactory. Of course, the ideal way is to grow the plants in small flower pots and when they have formed a ball of roots, set them in the garden. The next best is to grow them in seed pans or flats (shallow boxes) in which they should be set several inches apart as soon as large enough to handle, and in which they should be allowed to grow for a few weeks, to form a mass of roots. When these plants are to be set in the garden they should be broken apart by hand with as little loss of roots as possible.

[**Illustration: Center Row Hand Cultivator**]

The Labiatae and the Umbellifer are the names of these two coteries, the former of which includes the sages, mints, and their cousins, and the latter of which includes the parsleys and their kin. All of the significant leaf herbs, except for tarragon, which belongs to the Composite, parsley, and a few of its relatives that have abandoned their ranks, belong to the Labiate, and all of the herbs whose seeds are employed for flavoring, with rare exceptions, belong to the Umbellifer. Fennel-flower, a member of the natural order Ranunculaceae, or the crowfoot family, is a candidate for membership in the seed sodality; costmary and southernwood, both members of the Composit; are interested in joining the leaf faction; and rue, a member of the Rutaceae; and tansy, a member of the Composite, despite being expelled for their brazenness and bad breeding, occasionally reenter the territory of the leaf A composite named Marigold creates the most exclusive club of all by herself. It has not accepted any new members! There also don't seem to be any candidates.

The important members of the Labiatæ are:

Sage (Salvia officinalis, Linn.).
Savory (Satureja hortensis, Linn.).
Savory, winter (Satureja montana, Linn.).
Thyme (Thymus vulgaris, Linn.).
Marjoram (Origanum Marjoram; O. Onites, Linn.; and
M. vulgare, Linn.).
Balm (Melissa officinalis, Linn.).
Basil (Ocimum Basilicum, Linn., and O. minimum, Linn.).
Spearmint (Mentha spicata, Linn., or M. viridis, Linn.).
Peppermint (Mentha Piperita, Linn.).
Rosemary (Rosmarinus officinalis, Linn.).
Clary (Salvia Sclarea, Linn.).
Pennyroyal (Mentha Pulegium, Linn.).
Horehound (Marrubium vulgare, Linn.).
Hyssop (Hyssopus vulgaris, Linn.).
Catnip (Nepeta Cataria, Linn.).
Lavender (Lavandula vera, D. C.; L. spica, D. C.).

These plants, which are mostly natives of mild climates of the old world, are characterized by having square stems; opposite, simple leaves and branches; and more or less two-lipped flowers that appear in the axils of the leaves, occasionally alone, but usually several together, forming little whorls, which often compose loose or compact spikes or racemes. Each fertile blossom is followed by four little seed-like fruits in the bottom of the calyx, which remain attached to the plant. The foliage is generally plentifully dotted with minute glands that contain volatile oil, upon which depends the aroma and piquancy peculiar to the individual species.

The leading species of the Umbelliferæ are:

Parsley (Carum Petroselinum, Benth. and Hook.).
Dill (Anethum graveolens, Linn.).
Fennel (Foeniculum officinale, Linn.).
Angelica (Archangelica officinalis, Hoof.).
Anise (Pimpinella anisum, Linn.).
Caraway (Carum carvi, Linn.).
Coriander (Coriandrum sativum, Linn.).
Chervil (Scandix Cerefolium, Linn.).
Cumin or Cummin (Cuminum Cyminum, Linn.).
Lovage (Levisticum officinale, Koch.).
Samphire (Crithmum maritimum, Linn.).

[Illustration: Sage, the Leading Herb for Duck and Goose Dressing]

Sage is typically grown by market gardeners as a secondary crop. As a result, they grow the plants in nursery beds. Very early in the spring, the seed is sown, not thicker than previously described, but in rows that are typically 6 to 9 inches apart. The seedlings are nurtured from the beginning and encouraged to develop stockily. The first summer vegetable sowings will have been marketed by late May or early June, and the land will be prepared for the sage. After preparing the soil, sage seedlings are typically replanted 6 to 8 inches apart. Up until the sage takes possession, clean cultivation is maintained. The alternative plants are cut, bunched, and sold when they meet, which normally occurs in late August.

The plants in the rows should initially not stand closer than 2 inches apart for cultivation with hand-wheel hoes. Each second one should be removed as soon as they contact, and this procedure should be repeated until, when grown commercially, each alternate row has been eliminated. The plants should also be spaced 12 to 15 inches apart. The rows will need to be spaced apart even further for cultivation by a horse; the typical range is 18 to 24 inches. Sage typically comes after field-grown lettuce, early peas, or early cabbage when it is farmed on a large scale. Sage plants have a good chance of surviving mild winters if they are not pruned too closely or too late in the season.

EXPERIENCE

I wanted to cultivate a lot of my herbs and spices because I'm experimenting with an organic diet, but I wasn't sure where to start. This book was a nice find for me because it was brief and to the point. I quickly picked up what I needed to know, and I'm already organizing my garden for this year. I'm happy that I can use the herbs I'm growing at home rather than having to go to the store because of many of the recipes... called for a lot of the herbs I was growing.

I hope this ebook has a great impact on you as you have gained some important knowledge on culinary Herbs.

www.ingramcontent.com/pod-product-compliance
Lightning Source LLC
LaVergne TN
LVHW021356160826
845679LV00008B/1642

* 9 7 9 8 3 6 4 8 8 1 4 9 6 *